6p

D1643897

This book belongs to

Lois

Barbie

in

The Frog Prince

Illustrations by
Christian Musselman and Lily Glass

EGMONT

EGMONT
We bring stories to life

This edition published in Great Britain 2008
by Egmont UK Limited
239 Kensington High Street, London W8 6SA

BARBIE and associated trademarks and trade dress are owned by,
and used under licence from, Mattel, Inc.
© 2007 Mattel, Inc.

1 3 5 7 9 10 8 6 4 2

Printed in China

All rights reserved. No part of this publication may be reproduced, stored in a retrieval system,
or transmitted, in any form or by any means, electronic, mechanical, photocopying, recording or
otherwise, without the prior permission of the publisher and copyright owner.

Hello, I'm Amelia, Princess of Arcadia.

This is a story about how I lost my golden ball. When a frog helped me to get it back, I learned an important lesson about friendship . . .

At the bottom of the royal garden, under the shade of a lime tree, was a little pond surrounded by tall reeds and bulrushes.

In the summer, Princess Amelia sat on its daisy-covered banks for hours every day.

She admired the dragonflies as they skimmed over the lily cups, and counted the silvery fish as they darted among the dark weeds.

A lonely frog lived in the pond. He spent his days swimming through the reeds, and waiting for Princess Amelia to come by. He admired her pretty face and wished he could be her friend.

One day, the frog looked out from between the bulrushes to see Princess Amelia playing catch with a golden ball.

"Fetch, Truffle!" she cried, and her puppy balanced the ball on the end of his nose.

Amelia threw the ball again, but Truffle missed it. It bounced and rolled into the pond, where it bobbed on the water.

"Oh dear!" cried Amelia. She tried to reach the golden ball from the stepping stones, but they were too slippery.

Truffle splashed into the water, but before he reached the ball it started sinking.

It slid right down out of sight and settled on the muddy bottom.

Princess Amelia flopped down on the bank and cried into her lacy handkerchief.

The frog felt very upset and hopped over to talk to her.

"Don't be sad, princess," he croaked softly.

"I've lost my golden ball," she sobbed. "I'll give you my crown and my ruby ring if you fetch it for me."

"I don't want your jewels," said the frog. "But I would like to be your friend."

Princess Amelia wasn't sure about having a new friend, but Truffle gave the frog a happy lick. Reluctantly, Princess Amelia agreed to the arrangement.

The frog dived down, and reappeared holding the sparkling golden ball.

"Oh, thank you," said the princess happily. She threw the ball to Truffle as they ran off towards the palace.

"Wait!" croaked the frog, hopping after her.

A princess must keep her word. So, trying not to shudder, Princess Amelia carefully picked up the frog and put him in her pocket.

When they arrived at the palace, she dropped him into the courtyard fountain.

"Stay there till I come to get you," she said.

The frog didn't like the small, chilly fountain. He waited all day, but Princess Amelia didn't come to see him.

So the frog splashed down from level to level of the old fountain. He lowered himself to the ground on a string of weed, and hopped up the 100 steps of the grand stairway. He slowly climbed the bell rope and lifted the heavy knocker.

Princess Amelia's butler wouldn't let the frog inside. But Truffle took pity on him, and carried him to the banquet hall.

Amelia wasn't very pleased to see a slimy little frog in her lovely palace!

"Shoo!" she told him angrily.

"You promised you would be my friend!" the frog complained sadly.

Amelia knew a princess must keep her word.

"Very well," she said. "But if you're going to be my friend, you will have to dress like a little prince."

So the maid brought an elegant sugar bowl, and the frog took a champagne bath in it.

The court tailor took his measurements, and made him a little green suit and black velvet slippers.

He put a lily-shaped coronet on his head, and a tiny ruby on his finger.

Now he was the finest-looking frog in the whole kingdom!

"I'm hungry," said the frog. "I want to sit next to you. I want to eat from your silver plate and drink from your crystal cup."

Princess Amelia perched him on a huge pile of cushions in the chair beside her. He ate politely, one crumb at a time, and drank from her glass without spilling a drop.

"I need to sleep now," he said at last. "Take me to your bedroom."

The princess put him in a tiny bed with a tasselled cushion and blanket. But that wasn't enough for the frog.

"What's the matter?" demanded Princess Amelia angrily. "After everything I've given you, what more could you want?"

"You've forgotten to give me a goodnight kiss," said the frog.

"Princesses don't kiss frogs!" cried Princess Amelia in horror.

"Kiss me, and I'll go away forever," promised the frog.

So Princess Amelia forced herself to give the frog a quick peck.

To her amazement, he turned into a handsome prince, dressed in robes of emerald green with a sparkling ruby ring on his finger.

From then on, Princess Amelia and Prince Fergus were the best of friends!

Magical titles in this series:

Look out for more enchanting tales to add to your collection!